Trickety Track

My friend bought me a ticket for the Trickety Track.
"Trickety Track!" I said.

"What's that?"

"It's the silliest ride you've ever been on.

The guard checked our tickets and showed us in.

Chuff chuff,

toot

TRAIN
DEPARTS
AT
3 O'clock

toot!

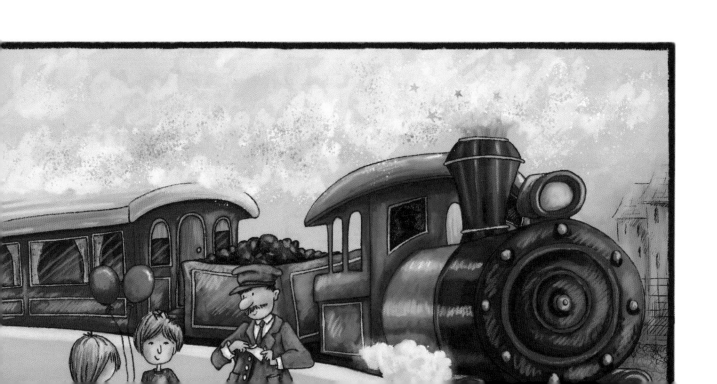

The train pulled away with a **chugga choo choo,**
when ants in pants brought us tea for two!
They laid down the cups with a

Ching-a-ching chong!

Moving in time to the train's rhythmic song.

Trickety Track, Trickety Track,

Where are we going?
We're not going back!

An elephant, a lion, and a kangaroo!

The elephant **wiggled** his great long trunk,
and reached for the tea which he promptly drunk!
While kangaroo, lion and I, leapfrogged along,
listening once more to the train's rhythmic song.

Trickety Track, Trickety Track,

Where are we going?
We're not going back!

A mermaid along with the **sea**!

She flipped up her tail, brought it down with a splash,
creating **huge** waves, which we surfed in a **flash**

We surfed to the shore
as the waves rolled along,
listening once more
to the train's rhythmic song!

Trickety Track, Trickety Track,

Where are we going?
We're not going back!

A monkey with a dog that **flew**!

Monkey magicked us wings,
and we went for a fly.

Looping

the loop

Trickety Track, Trickety Track,

Where are we going?
We're not going back!

And a penguin peeked in!

"Am I too late?
Did the party begin?

I was sure I was faster than a
flapping fin!"

"No penguin, you're just in time.

Everyone ate as we **chuffed, chuffed** along,
listening once more to the train's rhythmic song.

Trickety Track, Trickety Track,

Where are we going?

We're back!

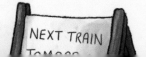

NEXT TRAIN